Amaranthine and Other Stories

Amaranthine and Other Stories

Erik Hofstatter

FOR AKONA

Contents

The Birthing Tub

EAN PEELED a single strand of stringy, russet hair from his shoulder and caressed it between his wrinkled fingers. The bathroom tiles were decorated with grimy cracks. He stuck the hair on the tile, next to the others. Tilting his head, he studied the tokens with sorrow in his eyes. It seemed like the entwined hairs formed a mysterious map. *A map to a better life*, he wished. The hair did not belong to him, yet they lurked all over the cottage, sometimes in the most unlikely of places. Farewell gifts from Magda. How long has she been gone? Months? Years? Sean could hardly remember. She had robbed him of logic, as well as his heart. Nothing made sense anymore. Her departure created a void. The joy of living evaporated along with her. Time ceased to exist. Sean inhaled and submerged his head, bathing in the serenity of underwater silence. It brought him a temporary peace. He thought about Eli and how he was born in this very tub. Witnessing his birth was one of the happiest days of Sean's life. He had to stay strong, if not for himself then for Eli. As long as he had Eli, he would find the strength to carry on living.

He exited the bath and reached for a stained towel. It smelled of neglect—dirt and mould. Sean could not remember the last time he swapped it. Another one of Magda's hairs was wrapped around his wrist like a constrictor. *You always were a snake,* Sean thought, uncoiling the cruel reminder and flushing it down the toilet—if only he could flush his feelings along with it. He caught a glimpse of his skeletal reflection in the steamed mirror, resisting the urge to wipe it and reveal the full horror of his anorexic body. No, he already accepted his Auschwitz appearance. No need to torment himself further. There was nothing he could do. Sean had a beastly appetite, yet the consumed nutrients simply vanished. Magda used to envy his rapid metabolism. "What's your secret? You can eat anything you like without gaining a pound!" she said.

Body dried, he slipped on his robe. A startled moth flew out of the garment. Sean clapped his hands, annihilating the insect with feline reflexes. *Bastard! I'll teach you to eat material from my robe*! He washed his palms, watching the golden dust dissipate into the sink. Entering the kitchenette, he removed the chicken breasts from the freezer. What day was it? Tuesday. No, Thursday! It did not matter to Sean. His life had become a routine. Routine was important. After Magda's abandonment, routine kept him sane. The microwave broke last month. It dawned on him how much time had passed since he'd last ventured outside. *Shit, has it been that long already?* Sean accepted a voluntary redundancy package the company offered him. He paid the rent several months in advance and stocked up on food. Frozen chicken, rice, beans, spaghetti, tuna, various soups—canned goods mostly. Quitting his job seemed irrelevant. His life had transformed into a game of dominoes since Magda left him.

She was the tip of the iceberg. She was the avalanche that buried his existence. Now he had to dig himself out of the snow. At least he had Eli. The loyal Eli. He would never desert him.

He sliced through the bag. The knife was blunt. Sean realized it would've been easier to rip the bag open with his fingers. Prevailing at last, he removed a piece of chicken. It still felt solid, even after leaving it in the sink to defrost for fifteen minutes. *Oh, well. The damn thing will defrost when it's cooking*, he thought. Soon, the air in the kitchenette carried a smell of frying onions. Sean stirred it and returned his attention to the frozen meat. He reached for a sharper knife and began to cut his dinner into little squares, leaning on the blade with every ounce of his puny weight. The onion made his eyes water. Why was he still bothering with that fucking thing? Did he care about taste? All the accoutrements and exotic spices? No. His life was about survival now. Fuck the spices. But then he remembered why he still fried the onion. Because Magda told him so. "Every delicious dish starts with fried onions. That's the base," she explained. Her Polish creations often made him salivate. Sean did not argue with her culinary reasoning. Now he felt like tossing the brown mishmash into the bin. The wok trembled in his hands. No, frying the onion was part of the routine. He must stick to the routine.

Since the turbulent separation, Sean devoured an identical meal every night. Chicken breast with brown rice. If he felt brave enough, he hazarded a little honey or mustard to enrich the dish. Not tonight. He stared into the wok, stirring the mixture absent-mindedly. How long was the chicken cooking? Five minutes? Ten? Without a clock in the kitchenette, he could not tell. He did not care, either. Food poisoning was the least of his worries. Magda had left him. That's what mattered. Sean poked the chicken with a wooden spoon. The texture seemed rubbery. *Maybe a minute or two longer*, he thought. Drops of burning oil landed on his knuckles, a result of over-vigorous stirring. "Cock!" he shouted out loud, shaking his hand through the air. The rice boiled. He removed the plastic sack with a fork, letting the excess water drip into the sink. Satisfied, he emptied the contents onto his plate. Sean gave the meat a final stir and scraped it on top of his rice.

The chicken was undercooked. Sean chewed the tasteless grub from side to side in his mouth, resisting the urge to spit it out. *You must keep your strength up. It's about survival. The pain will fade. You must eat*, he encouraged himself. Sean split the next piece in half with his fork. The shades of pink were undeniable. He carried on munching. It was all routine, even the undercooked meat. Every night he attempted to prepare the chicken thoroughly, every night he failed. "You're a failure!" Magda said to him. More than once. His reply remained the same. "Only in your eyes."

"Only in your eyes," he muttered again. She often smirked. He hated that fucking smirk. It irritated him more than words. The contempt on her lips. The superiority in her eyes. Her slyness had frightened him from the beginning. It also served as a magnet. Magda's intelligence was an attractive quality he could not resist.

"Get out of my fucking head!" he roared.

He needed a distraction. He needed Eli. He could always talk to Eli. Eli possessed the ability to vanquish these unwanted emotions. After dinner, Sean poured himself a generous glass of whiskey and collapsed into his Chesterfield chair. The chair was his throne—his sanctuary. It provided a sense of invincibility.

When he presided in his chair, even Magda could not challenge his authority. He sniffed the leather before leaning towards the aquarium—tapping a nail on the glass and addressing the floating thing within.

"I love you, Eli. You're my last friend on this doomed planet. How would I cope without you?"

The segmented body of the creature appeared lifeless. It nestled at the bottom of the tank, white and flat. He marvelled at the great length. Eli measured at least three and a half meters. Sean read that they developed at a rapid pace. Certain articles even claimed 1cm growth every hour. When Sean gave birth to him in the tub, Eli was already at an impressive size. He saluted his offspring and gulped down the amber liquid. Sean relaxed in his seat and reminisced back to that glorious day. His eyes lingered over the empty spaces she once occupied. Suddenly, he felt dirty. From the angry sex no doubt. Magda suggested it. "Fancy some break up sex? No strings attached?" she said. Always the temptress. She enjoyed torturing him, toying with his feelings until the bitter end. He nodded, intrigued by the lustful proposition.

Sean slipped his pants down, already hard. Magda stepped towards him, raising her skirt. The absence of underwear suggested she planned this in advance—even anticipating his answer. She did not kiss him. Instead, she reached for his cock and impaled herself on his erection. The sudden penetration swept his breath away. He experienced a new feeling there and then—a feeling of violation. Why was she doing this to him? Why the deviant treatment? She rode him with hate pouring out of her eyes. His heart ached with every thrust of her hips. After the farewell coitus, Magda raised herself from his lap and left the room. No words were spoken. No words were needed. She slammed the door behind her, disappearing from his life forever—in search of her own fortunes. What exactly was she searching for? Sean did not know. He only guessed that Magda searched for something more—for something he could not provide.

Sean lay in the bathtub, scrubbing his scrawny body, washing away Magda's scent with unnecessary force. The brush etched into his raw skin, leaving traces of crimson lines. Then it happened. His stomach cramped. The excruciating pain left him paralysed. *That fucking chicken*, he thought, holding his belly. He wanted to jump out of the tub and race to the nearby toilet, but Sean could not straighten his body. Beads of sweat formed on his forehead. Jaw clenched, he fought until the very end. All in vain. He shut his eyes and let go. Sean heard bubbles rising from beneath the water. He felt his stomach deflate. The corner of his mouth twisted into a grimace of relief. It was over.

Then the whiff of faeces polluted the air. It smelled like a corpse left to rot in the Saharan sun. No, it smelled far worse. Sean's eyes snapped wide open. He was bathed in a brown river of diarrhoea. Regurgitating, he pinched his nose. Something else floated in the tub with him. He refocused and locked his eyeballs on the intruder. The thing was wrapped around a solid chunk of shit. Sean hesitated before scooping it up with utter disgust. He separated it from his excrement, the liquid stool trickling down his wrist. The thing was long and thin, like a spaghetti—except the colour. It was pure white. It wiggled and wrapped itself around Sean's index finger. He blinked, turning his hand from side to side, observing the creature that just swam out of his asshole.

"Aren't you a beauty? I shall call you Eli," he said to it.

Sean vacated the aquarium by flushing Magda's goldfish down the toilet. Eli needed a new home. He gently carried the parasite and dropped him in the water. It sank to the bottom. It all seemed like aeons ago.

Sean rubbed the chair, his mind whizzing through memories. He attempted to banish the pain Magda's betrayal created. Past no longer mattered. He had to focus on the moment and live in the present. Focus on Eli. Nourish and look after him. Magda did not deserve his love, but Eli did.

"Do you remember when you were born? What a beautiful day that was. My beloved Magda might be gone, but you'll always be my son. Never forget that."

A proud grin spread across his features as he gazed at Eli, floating in the water. He produced another life. It *came* out of him. Eli was so much more than an intestinal worm, he was Sean's son. His stomach cramped again, the pain spreading through his bowels—the tapeworms slowly crippling him. Sean raised himself from the chair, hunched over like a pensioner. He tapped the glass of the aquarium.

"Hope you're ready, Eli. When I come back, I might have a little brother for you," he said, heading towards the toilet.

Tristan's Equation

RISTAN'S EYES snapped shut. His clammy palms cupped over his ears—slowly anticipating the dreadful announcement. Every three minutes for the last four hours, the transistor radio located on the top shelf (and out of his short reach) would broadcast a sequence of numbers. A sequence that he loathed—a sequence that drove him insane.

The cacophonous speaker rattled and a thunderous voice proclaimed the following digits:

(15,5,8, 9 – 10)

Tristan pressed harder on his ears. Silence dominated all. The broadcast was over for the next three minutes. Eight-year old Tristan paced around the white room.

Why are they repeating these numbers? What do they mean? Why am I here? What do they want me to do?

He approached the mahogany desk, covered with all sorts of mathematical equations and calculations.

He picked up one of the papers and looked at it again. It showed the following diagram:

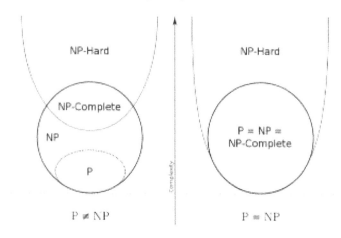

Tristan blinked, attempting to re-focus his eyes. The drawing made no sense no matter how long or hard he stared at it. The strict voice repeated again:

(15,5,8, 9 – 10)

No! Please, no more...

Tristan started to weep.

Where is mom? Where is dad? Why am I all alone here?

He tried to peek into the circular mirror on the east wall but it towered over him and he could not see himself.

Frustrated, he pulled a chair from the desk and climbed on it—gazing upon his own reflection in the mirror. The tips of his fingers traced the elongated scar on the top of his scalp.

I can't remember how I got this...

The tissue of the scar felt callous, an injury sustained quite some time ago. He jumped down from the chair and looked at the bulb, hanging from the ceiling. It shattered violently—the shards missing his left eye by an inch. Tristan was cloaked by darkness.

He crawled under the desk, crying and hugging his knees. The speaker rattled once again, the electro-magnetic signals echoing around the room:

(15,5,8, 9 – 10)

Tristan felt consumed by the invisible waves. The sound in the blackness terrified him even more. He repeated the sequence in his head, a feeble attempt at deciphering the hidden meaning of the numbers. He was good with numbers. His parents said so.

"You're a very special boy," his mother had often reminded him.

Tristan wiped the tears from his eyes and inhaled. No, the sequence was meaningless. But what if it's not about the numbers themselves?

What if there's something else, hidden in the me-chanical waves? A code? A signal? Did I hear a trace of beeps behind that voice? It sounded like a Morse code? But from who? Who is transmitting these num-bers and why?

All these questions clouded his ability to concen-trate and he shuddered with despair. His eyes slowly adjusted to the darkness and he saw a shadow of footsteps in the gap underneath the door.

They swung open. Tristan lifted his arm, shielding his eyes from the cruel light.

"Tristan? Where are you?"

The boy hesitated. He did not recognize the voice. But then, unable to hide in fear any longer—he crawled forward, sobbing and trembling.

"Oh, dear! What are you doing under the table? Why is this not working?" Asked the man, flipping the light switch up and down.

Tristan ran towards him, tears trickling down his cheeks once again. He hugged the man, burying his face in his white coat—not caring that he was a stranger.

"There, there, no need to cry. I see the light bulb exploded," said Dr. Guttridge, patting Tristan on the head. "I'm so sorry, Tristan. Nurse Patel was meant to check up on you every hour but clearly she's forgotten."

The broadcast began yet again:
(15,5,8, 9 – 10)
Dr. Guttridge walked over to the small radio, switching it off.

"What do those numbers mean? Who are you? Why am I here?" asked Tristan.

Dr. Guttridge squeezed his shoulder. "I'm ever so sorry, Tristan. As I explained before, nurse Patel was instructed to keep an eye on you every hour or so, to answer any questions you might have and to remind you of your task."

"My task?"

Dr. Guttridge gestured towards the chair and Tristan sat down.

"Your task, Tristan, was to solve the P versus NP problem—an unsolved problem in computer science. You're a very special boy, Tristan. Your IQ is 138 and you're a brilliant mathematician therefore your parents decided that you should try to resolve it."

"Why?"

"The unsolved problem carries a price tag of $1,000,000 to whoever cracks it. I'd imagine that motivated your parents," said Dr. Guttridge.

Tristan did not pick up on the doctor's sarcasm.

"But why don't I remember any of this?"

"Well, you see, you suffered a traumatizing injury as a baby—hence the scar on your head. It's because of this injury, that you lost the ability to create new memories. The condition is called *Anterograde Amnesia*."

Tristan sat in silence, his mouth partially opened.

"Where are my parents?"

"They're waiting for you in the hallway."

The boy started walking towards the door and the doctor placed an arm around his shoulder.

"I failed," Tristan confessed with his head bowed.

Dr. Guttridge smiled in return. "Do not trouble yourself, Tristan. The P versus NP problem is one of *seven* Millennium Prize Problems. There are always the other six."

Tristan's eyes opened and he examined the wrinkled reflection staring back at him from the mirror. He no longer needed a chair to climb onto.

Amaranthine

"Y OUR BOOK will be ready for collection next week," I informed Mr Johnson, one of my new clients. He was an older man, perhaps in his sixties but looked like someone who took great pride in their appearance.

"Can't it be done sooner?" He frowned and pierced me with a sharp glance.

I shook my head in defeat, "please, you must understand that this is a delicate custom order and special attention to detail is required. . . "

"Very well, call me when it's done!" Mr Johnson barked and marched out of my shop.

Ah yes, my emporium of odd curiosities. I inherited it from my father, who was a book binder for most of his life. In his declining years, he opened a small bookshop of his own but sadly didn't live long enough to see it prosper. A heart attack killed him six months later. He was swiftly cremated and I displayed the urn in the shop to keep his memory alive. I tried my best to keep the business going but there's not much hope for independent bookshops or rookie businessmen these days. The shop was losing money rapidly and I knew that drastic change was needed.

I missed my father and wished daily that he was still alive, if only to offer guidance. I didn't want to let him down by bankrupting the shop he'd worked so hard for. I had to do something. . . innovative.

The bell above the door rang and a new figure approached the reception—a lanky woman with jet black hair, pale skin and cherry red lipstick. "I trust you received my e-mail," she began in a foreign accent.

"I did indeed, you must be Ms Muller," I replied whilst scrolling down the contents on my monitor.

The woman revealed a smile of crooked teeth.

"That's right, I brought you the materials you requested," she said and handed me a plastic bag smeared with blood.

I stared at the bag, mildly surprised at the poor presentation and total lack of care.

"Erm, thank you. As you know, this is a special custom order and due to our recent hectic schedule—your order will take several weeks."

Unlike Mr Johnson, Ms Muller seemed content with the lead time.

"That's perfectly understandable," she said and removed her dark sunglasses, "as you're the only specialist in the area. I'll be in touch."

She departed and I was glad to watch her leave, as her Gothic presence had created a certain sense of melancholy in the shop.

I snatched the plastic bag and tied a tag around it with Ms Muller's name.

Where was I? Oh, yes! I had to do something innovative to reverse my fortunes. The torment of my father's death provided inspiration for my new business expansion. I wanted to keep him with me at all times but his ashes weren't enough. . .

What if cremation wasn't the only method of keeping your loved ones with you? What if you could actually keep a *piece* of them? An everlasting token that you could touch and *feel*. . .

A new idea was born, and my Lord, how the clients poured in!

Of course officially, I was just an average shop owner and had to keep up legit appearances but on a black market, behind the scenes I was quite a celebrity for my unique services.

The technique itself was popular in the 16th century and I was determined to revive the trend, as book binding ran in the family after all. Anthropodermic bibliopegy, or the practice of binding books in human skin was my forte and I assure you—the practice is in high demand. . . even today.

The Wandering Pilgrim

 IS CRYSTAL clear eyes bore into hers. Alexandra sat on a mahogany settee, hands folded in her lap—mesmerised by his stare. Nonchalantly, she stood to slip out of her silky gown, his melodic voice commanding so. A wet tongue slithered over her half-erect nipple. The mysterious wanderer uttered words of instruction whilst she obeyed, spellbound.

His voice infatuated, penetrated every thought. Under his dark tunic, the monk stroked his member, feeling it grow in his calloused palm. The flame of the candle swayed with his rhythmic moaning. Her mental state altered, she registered the mystic's unflinching eyes as they drank her exposed flesh. Soon, his volcano erupted with burning drops landing as far as her bosoms.

Still she sat, eyes wide open and tongue silent. Grigori wiped away the sloppy, white explosion with his soiled tunic—his devilish gaze probing her soul. He clicked his fingers. A satisfied grin stretched across his bearded face. Alexandra, the last Tsaritsa of Russia, awoke from hypnosis. She blinked then gasped, shocked at the sight of her own nudity.

"What have you done to me?" she asked.

His pupils dilated as he shifted away from the candlelight and closer to her face. Kneeling, the mad monk clutched her quivering knees. "My child, those who deliberately commit fornication and repent bitterly will be closer to God," he answered.

The Deep End

HE TREADED water in the deep end, observing screaming brats with quiet distaste. They circled the pool, pushing, splashing and causing havoc. Eva's eyes lingered on Sophie. She swam by herself in the abandoned corner of the shallow pool, dunking her head beneath the water and emerging again after several seconds like a seal pup.

Eva rubbed her forehead, blaming the migraine on the over-chlorinated water. She despised swimming. Only Toby, the charismatic young lifeguard she befriended, made the weekly ordeal worthwhile. He patrolled the other side of the pool now, his eyes alert and ready for action. She admired his trapezius muscles, bursting out of his aureolin T-shirt and his masculine thighs, concealed beneath the scarlet shorts.

To quench her lust, she sank below the surface like an anchor, feeling the increased pressure as her feet brushed against the bottom of the pool. Eva opened her eyes under water, bathing in the blissful silence, watching the children's silhouettes kicking but no longer screaming. The water drowned their voices.

One of the drains caught her eye. A long tuft of black hair, very much like her own, floated from the tiny hole. Her fingers stretched towards the entangled filament but she could hold her breath no longer.

When her head popped up, the baby-faced Toby beamed at her. The colour of the pool matched his eyes and she wondered what it would be like if she could bathe in them, swim in them, every day.

"Aren't you supposed to be watching Sophie instead of exploring the bottom of our pool?" He asked, crouching and chuckling.

Eva rested her elbows on the edge of the pool.

"Why do I need to watch her when you're here?" she said, producing her most seductive smile.

He sheepishly averted his eyes. Eva's sexy, melodic accent caused the embarrassment rather than her smile, which he also found agreeable. "You're not very passionate about your job, are you?"

"Honestly? No, I'm not. I only applied to be an *Au Pair* because I wanted to experience a different culture," said Eva, shrugging her shoulders, "Bulgaria is such a backward nation, full of simpletons and I always dreamed of visiting sophisticated countries like England or America. Of course I come from a poor family so my parents could never afford to finance my trip. A friend of mine recommended a student agency that specialised in placing young girls into families abroad, to help them with childcare, light cooking etcetera."

"So you're basically a servant?"

Eva frowned at the term. "I hate to admit it, but yeah. The agency also failed to mention how fucking spoiled this child was going to be. English kids are so poorly disciplined. That's the biggest cultural shock I had so far, I think. Bulgarian children might be poor but their lives are enriched with simple happiness and activities, like running around in a forest, climbing trees, playing games—not shacked up in their rooms, Skyping on their iPhones all day. Their parents are practically robbing them of childhood by supporting this brainwashing technology age we live in."

"I know what you mean," Toby sighed," I grew up like that. My folks are outdoorsy people too and most of my childhood was spent outside, playing sports. Guess it depends on the parents rather than nationalities."

"True," she nodded, "but Sophie *is* spoiled, plus she hates my guts. Gerard, her dad, told me that her mother died of leukaemia last year and obviously he needed domestic help. He works in London as some kind of a Sales Executive and is hardly ever home. He decided to hire an *Au Pair* because he also wanted his daughter to learn about other cultures. I taught her that the city I'm from is almost spelt the same as her name, *Sofia*. She liked that. I knew the job would entail cooking, cleaning, taking and collecting Sophie from school - but most people never read the small print, like washing Gerard's shit-smeared boxers."

Toby blew his whistle. "No running!" he yelled at the boys on the other side of the pool. The display of authority, the sudden change in his voice, that savage dominance made her heart skip a beat.

"Why does she hate you?" he countered, smiling down once more.

"Well, my theory is that she's jealous of the attention I get from Gerard. After the death of her mother, she got used to the fact that she was the centre of his universe. She didn't have to compete for his attention. But now, when she sees us joking, laughing together—she doesn't like it."

Eva glanced at the giant clock above the pool. "Shit! Is that the time? We're late! Gerard's picking us up today," she announced, climbing out of the pool.

"Okay, see you next Saturday?"

Eva nodded, collecting Sophie and smiling warmly. "By the way, you might want to check out your drains, there's loads of hair down there."

Her accent thickened and he failed to understand the full sentence but grinned anyway. His eyes devoured Eva's voluptuous body as she walked away.

Like a hen, pecking corn off the ground, Eva pecked dirty clothes off various places in Sophie's pink room, cursing quietly in Bulgarian. The little girl observed her slave, smirking.

"Did you have fun swimming today?" Eva asked, picking up a dirty sock.

"No, I don't want to go anymore. The pool scares me. Morgen scares me. He was mean to me today because of you. He hates you."

The tropical temperature in the room intensified Eva's on-going migraine. She sat on the bed, next to Sophie. "Who's Morgen? Why would he hate me?"

"He's my friend and he just does."

"But I've never even seen him!"

"It doesn't matter. He saw you. And he doesn't like you," Sophie mumbled.

"Who is he? One of the other kids? Perhaps you can introduce me to Morgen next week, if he's there, and I'll show him how nice I really am."

"I don't want to. He's scary. He's always there. . . in the pool."

"I'm sure he's not as scary as you think, Sophie. We'll talk to him next week. Now get in bed and I'll tuck you in."

Eva closed the door behind her and strolled into the not too distant living room. Why would Sophie say such horrible things to her? Was jealousy really the root of the problem? She searched her memory but did not recall seeing Sophie talking to anyone new. Perhaps she'd missed something while she was flirting with Toby?

Gerard nestled on the couch, his eyes spellbound by the telly. He did not even register Eva entering the room. She immediately knew why. A bottle of *Kraken*, his favourite black rum, stood on the table, a quarter already consumed.

She lingered there in the shadows, watching him. He looked sad. Eva assumed he still missed his wife. His static eyes seemed far away, the program mere background noise. After a while she realized it was the dancing flame of the candle that mesmerized him. She cleared her throat and sat next to him.

"Heeeey! There she is! How are you? How did the swimming go?" Gerard asked, his voice dulled with liquor.

"Fine, thanks. I see you're having fun by yourself," said Eva, trying not to sound bitter. Gerard fingered the glass on his lap. The high-pressured job, reflected in his many wrinkles, troubled her. She noticed his daily alcohol intake had increased, too.

"How can I have fun when you're not here?" He countered, giggling and sipping his sedative.

Eva removed the glass from his grasp. "Listen, we need to talk. It might not be the best time for it but I need to get it off my chest," she began, watching his eyes struggling to focus, "Sophie's been acting strange these last couple of weeks and she doesn't want to go swimming anymore. The pool scares her."

"Of course it scares her," Gerard mumbled, "she's nine years old. Every child is scared of water. They're scared of drowning."

"Well, she doesn't seem to be scared of drowning. Apparently she's scared of Morgen."

"Morgen? I take it that you're referring to one of the other kids and not the Welsh water spirit?" he grinned.

"Water spirit? What are you talking about?"

"I used to read stories to Sophie when she was little. . . about Morgens," he slurred. "They were known to lure men to their deaths by their sylphic beauty or with glimpses of underwater gardens with buildings of gold and crystal."

"Shut up, Gerard. This is important. I think she's not coping with this scenario very well, you know, us being together. She's obviously still upset about

Cynthia's death and is not comfortable with the idea of me replacing her mum."

"I know, I know, "he said, stroking her thigh, "but we're taking things slowly, aren't we? The longer you're around the more she'll get used to your presence and might accept the fact that you're a part of this family."

"And if she doesn't? Will you discard me like a piece of garbage?" she asked, raising her eyebrows.

"Look, it's obvious that Sophie loves you dearly and doesn't want to share you with anyone else, especially me. I wonder if she invented this Morgen character as a way to express her hatred for me. Or maybe she feels isolated so she created an imaginary friend. Sophie is a very solitary child; she's not interacting with the other kids as much as she should," Eva continued.

"There's nothing wrong with a bit of solitude. I was isolated as a child and I turned out fine. Isolation will give her the opportunity to read books; it will help her to focus on other things - significant things, not slacking outside and getting corrupted by outsiders. Maybe she's slightly jealous of us being together but she'll get over it soon enough, you'll see. Just ignore it," Gerard said, waving his hand dismissively.

Eva sighed and crossed her arms. Six months had passed since she became a part of this family and only two months since she began sleeping with Gerard.

She loved him, despite the shocking age gap. She preferred older men. They were wiser, more settled and definitely more skilled in the bedroom.

"Let me brush your hair," Gerard offered, out of the blue.

He adored her hair. They reminded him of the ethereal *Rapunzel*, from the fairy tale by brothers Grimm. *Rapunzel's* hair was so long that she could wrap it around a hook beside the window, dropping it down to the prince so he could climb up to her lonely tower, except they were blonde – not raven black like Eva's. Gerard ran the brush through her rich mane, sniffing a strand in his hand that still reeked of chlorine.

"I've got this awful premonition," said Eva suddenly.

"Don't be silly! Sophie likes you very much, as do I. She just needs a bit more time to adjust, that's all,"

Eva attempted a smile but it was not sincere. She dreamed the darkest of dreams that night.

They entered the swimming area and Eva's eyes immediately locked on the lifeguard seat. It wasn't Toby who sat on it. Disappointment spread through her like a plague of locusts. She grasped Sophie's hand in hers and walked towards the pool, avoiding a bunch of screaming kids who shoved past them.

"I'm scared, I don't want to swim today," Sophie groaned.

"What are you scared of? Of yes, I remember," Eva slapped her forehead, "you're scared of Morgen, right? Is he here today? Show him to me."

Sophie bowed her head, nibbling at her lower lip.

"He's always here. Hiding in the pool."

"Well, show me where he's hiding and we'll talk to him together," Eva offered.

"No, I'm scared. He might hurt you."

"I'm a big girl from a rough country, I can handle myself," she winked at Sophie.

"Maybe later,"

Sophie slipped out of her hand and bombed into the partially empty pool, a rarity on a Saturday afternoon. *Fine, have it your way as usual.*

Eva observed from a distance once again, leaving the girl to her own devices. She still contemplated how spoiled and pampered English children were. Nothing made her blood boil more than seeing a seven year old child spilling out of a pram.

She'd had no such luxury in Bulgaria. Her father made her walk everywhere as a child, only when her legs truly tired did he swing her onto his shoulders. But none of this pram shit. *Damn these parents and their selfishness! It's all about what's convenient for them, never mind the child.*

She began to get seriously bored and missed flirting with Toby. She missed his baby-face and blue eyes, his smile and good nature. Eva loved Gerard but Toby certainly was worth sinning for.

It started to get busy now. More mothers entered the pool with their offspring. Eva grinned at the scene unfolding before her eyes. The pool resembled a giant pot of children, crammed in, over-spilling, screaming and slowly roasting above the flames, if only she could be the imp and poke them with her fork.

"He wants to meet you now," Sophie declared, snapping Eva out of her reverie.

"Sorry, darling? Who wants to meet me?"

"Morgen. He's down there, waiting for you,"

Eva followed her finger, pointing towards the deep end of the pool.

"There's no one there, Sophie."

"Yes, there is. Morgen's there, hiding at the bottom,"

"You want us to swim to the deep end of the pool? That's not a good idea, honey. You're too young, you might drown,"

"But he's there, waiting for us!"

Eva blinked several times. What was wrong with this child? Was she winding her up? Was this all a big joke to her? Did Gerard put her up to this? Why would he? If this carried on, she would suggest to him that his daughter needed to see a psychiatrist. This surpassed normal behaviour.

"I tell you what," said Eva, levelling herself with Sophie, "you stay here, be a good girl and I'll dive down there and take a look, deal?"

Sophie thought about it for a split second. "Okay, but be careful! I don't know what he wants from you."

"Don't worry, darling. He probably wants to tell me in secret how beautiful you are and if he can have your number," Eva joked, disgusted with her attempt at flattery. *Yes, that's it. Spoil her even more. But I need to win her over somehow.*

"You take a seat over there on the bench and I'll be back in a minute, darling," she said, wrapping her in a giant Mickey Mouse towel like candyfloss on a stick.

Eva walked cautiously along the edge of the pool, right towards the end. She read the sign DEEP END – DEPTH 5m - as if to reassure herself that this was the right place. She stared into the water, watching tiny waves form on the surface.

The bottom appeared so close yet so far. It glittered in the light, inviting her, calling her. She wasn't the strongest swimmer but did not fear water.

She waved to Sophie and took a deep breath, diving into the pool with eyes open, swimming ever deeper towards the bottom. She held her nose and equalized her ears. The pressure surprised her, even at 5 metres.

Eva glided effortlessly along the bottom of the pool, looking in all directions and eager to find Sophie's mysterious friend. The filthy drain she noticed last week caught her attention again. She could no longer see any hair floating from it but decided to take a closer look anyway.

She swam towards it, running her fingers over the smooth surface of the opening. Eva gazed into it for a few seconds when she heard a feeble whisper behind her. She flipped around towards the sound, her long *Rapunzel* hair floating all around. Eva regretted not tying it up. The water revealed nothing but blurry images of children's legs.

The temperature of the pool dropped and soon she would run out of air. Eva began to surface but an invisible force yanked her hair from behind. Her heart hammered as she desperately struggled to turn around, realizing that her long hair must've got entangled in the drain. Panic kicked in. She could not breathe. She could not swim. She could not escape. She could only scream, and scream she did, although it wasn't really a scream but more of a yelp. Eva watched bubbles slip out from her mouth as she struggled to free herself. The water turned murkier and darkness swallowed all.

As instructed, Sophie sat on the bench, smiling and humming. She watched the minutes pass on the enormous clock above the pool. How long has it been now? Ten minutes? Maybe more?

A lifeguard noticed Sophie at last from his little tower. He climbed down and sat next to her.

"Hello, are you okay?"

"Yes, thank you," replied Sophie, like a good girl.

"A young girl like you should be accompanied by an adult at all times, you know? We don't want any drowning accidents. Where's your mother?"

"My mother's dead," answered Sophie, gazing at the clock and wondering if Morgen had succeeded.

Eucalyptus Grove

 "E PLOTTED the ceremony for six weeks," I confessed, avoiding the detective's judgemental glare and listening to his porcine snorts. With one hand, he rubbed his shiny forehead. With the other, his meaty fingers clutched the pen—scribbling with hectic strokes. "Go on, boy, tell me exactly what happened that night."

And so I did. I'd undergone a recent spiritual rebirth. I was a Christian now and had to confess my sins, right?

The three of us revered heavy metal, satanic bands in particular. James's basement was our chapel and we headbanged in there religiously after school. Cradle of Filth, Behemoth, Slayer, Dimmu Borgir—you name it. We worshipped the lyrics and basked in the subliminal darkness they invoked. We even dabbled in music ourselves. James pestered me and Randy to help him with the ritual. He claimed it would benefit our own band.

"How exactly?" Randy asked.

Postmortem blasted in the background as James lit a bowl of meth, his face disappearing in a cloud of blinding smoke.

"Think about it! We'd receive power from the Devil! He'd help us play the guitar even better! We'd gain more craziness to go professional, know what I mean?"

I didn't, but the speculation caught my curiosity.

"I marked the grave last night so you two douches are still up for it, yeah?" James said.

I took a blow of meth and relaxed, letting the ecstasy rush through my head—dominating the senses.

"Yeah, let's do it tonight. You got the equipment, right?" Randy said.

"Sure, sure." I nodded.

Under the cover of nightfall, we climbed over the chained cemetery gate—creeping along the edges of the graves like silent ninjas.

"Hey! Which grave are we robbing again? I can't see shit!" I whispered.

"Just follow me and shut up. I know where I'm going!" James said.

It was a moonless, pitch black night. I tripped and nearly fell.

"Watch your step, dumbass!"

Randy laughed behind me while I tried my best to remain silent. Branches snapped under my army boots and the whole place smelled of compost. Soon, we came to a halt.

"This is it right here," James pointed, "Hey, Randy! Pass me the shovel!"

Just when the shovel touched soil, the gate flew open and we heard mumbled voices approaching in the distance.

"Shit! What was that?" James hissed, dropping to his knees.

A cloud of torches crept towards us.

"I saw them climbing over the gate, officer, I'm sure the satanic punks are around here somewhere," an elderly voice said.

I grabbed Randy and all three of us hid behind a grave.

"Crap! Someone spotted us!" I whispered to James, trying not to shit my pants.

The voices grew nearer.

"They're probably vandalising graves; you have to catch these punks!"

I swallowed hard, my throat enflamed.

"We gotta jump over that wall behind us and get the hell outta here, otherwise we're screwed!" I said.

Randy looked left and right in panic, his neck almost spinning like an owl's.

"Alright, let's go!" James commanded and we sprinted to the wall, hidden under a sycamore.

It was a short barricade and we climbed over it with panic in our hearts.

My lungs were on fire when we finally stopped running.

"How the fuck did they know it was us?" I panted.

James wiped the sweat off his brow, "They didn't— they just guessed."

"They got the satanic part right," Randy grinned.

I stretched and brushed dirt off my knees.

"Well, since we can't dig up a corpse for our offering, I say we go with Plan B. More extreme but definitely more fun. What do you say, boys? Randy and I will bring the tools. James—bring ganja and Eden," I said.

James, still panting and coughing replied: "Cool, man. We're on for next Friday, yeah?"

"Absolutely!" I said.

Eden, our whiny fifteen-year-old classmate. I failed to grasp what James ever saw in her.

"She's a virgin with blonde hair and blue eyes— what more do you want?" he winked.

We all rendezvoused at eucalyptus grove that Friday evening. James and Eden rolling on the grass, passing a doobie between them.

"Hey boys!" Eden said, nipping her finger and attempting a seductive smile. I loathed her and the purity she represented.

"Hi," I uttered—the simple greeting tasting like ash.

Randy towered beside me, staring at her boobs— drooling.

"Got the stuff?" James asked, excitement leaking out of his voice.

I nodded, grinning. "We sure have."

Slayer's *Dead Skin Mask* thundered from James's truck whilst the sun disappeared from the horizon. Eucalyptus grove was suddenly cloaked by shadows.

Eden's giggles irritated me. I grew impatient.

"Are we doing this shit or what?"

"Doing what?" Eden asked, obtuse and still giggling.

James slid from the bonnet of his truck, edging closer to Eden—rubbing her shoulders and whispering in her ear, "Sweetheart, you know how much we *adore* Slayer, right? We gathered here tonight with a single intention—to offer a pure sacrifice. . . "

Eden, glued to the spot—confusion smudging her naïve face—blinked. She smelled the weed on his breath and scowled.

"Sacrifice? To who? Who are we sacrificing?"

"We need to empower our music and you're gonna help us!" I said.

With a sadistic grin, James removed the belt from his camouflage shorts. He wrapped the ends around his bruised knuckles and flipped the belt over Eden's head with rapid motion—pulling and strangling. A shriek escaped, then she gasped—wriggling like a worm. Eden kicked her feet, struggling but failing to compete with James's brutal strength.

Randy and I observed. A patch of urine soaked her trousers while we watched—transfixed. Colour drained from Eden's face and adrenaline coursed through our veins. We felt euphoric.

"Whatcha waitin' for? Don't just stand there! *Do* it!" James barked whilst the puny girl choked, her feeble arms reaching out to us—desperation cascading from her eyes.

I yanked the hunting knife from my rucksack—launching at her neck—stabbing again and again and again. Like warm butter, the blade sank into her tender flesh.

Eden's knees crumbled and she collapsed on the ground—blood spraying from her jugular vein.

"Check it out, James! It's *Raining Blood*!" I pointed at her neck—laughing hysterically. *Raining Blood* was one of our all-time favourite Slayer songs. James high-fived me.

Our chortling spread across eucalyptus grove like a storm of locusts.

She whimpered on the ground, wriggling like a snake shedding its skin—choking on her own fluids.

"God...help!" Eden pleaded, blood splashing between her fingers.

Nothing happened so she called for her mummy instead. Pathetic cunt.

I wiped the blade on my sleeve and handed the knife to Randy.

"Put the bitch out of her misery," I instructed.

Randy's eyes sparkled with enthusiasm. He climbed on top of her almost limp body, watching blood pour out of the multiple wounds.

"There's still room here, look," he said, sinking the blade into Eden's neck once more.

Miraculously, the bitch coughed more blood. Randy and I had stabbed her at least twelve times and the cunt still breathed. How was that possible?

We smoked another spliff, glancing at Eden twitching on the ground, her hands flexing slowly—life fading from her eyes.

"I sure could use a beer right now," James said.

"Do you think she's dead yet?" I countered.

"Dunno, check her pulse."

I kneeled over the frail body, pressing two fingers on the debris that used to be her neck. No signs of life. At last, the cock tease was dead.

"Who'll take the first turn?" Randy said, unbuttoning his jeans and stroking his erection.

"You never had a chance with her when she was alive, might as well make the best of it now that she's dead," I chuckled, slapping his shoulder.

"Go for it, kid. You've earned it!" James encouraged.

Randy yelped in triumph, straddling her. He rolled up her white T-shirt—now dyed blood red and cut off her bra.

"I bet that's the first pair of tits you've seen, buddy, not counting your mom's!" James joked.

Our youngest accomplice groaned in pleasure, too infatuated with his prize to answer.

We ravaged Eden's tepid corpse that night, all three of us taking turns, and buried her pale body underneath a secluded eucalyptus.

"Don't bury her too deep," Randy whined. "I want to come back later and have another go!"

The moonlight illuminated our path as we strolled back to the truck.

"We gotta burn our clothes," James suggested, examining the bloodstains on his shirt.

"Damn right! Good thing I brought extra clothes for all of us," I said.

James drove us to his house and we headbanged to Slayer until the crack of dawn.

"What happened next?" prompted the detective, interrupting my train of thought.

I shifted in the wobbly chair. "Let's see. . . it happened eight months ago—my memory is vague!"

I caught a glint of doubt in his eyes then, as if he'd misheard.

"What do you think happened, genius? We left her out there to rot in the goddamn ground," I said.

The detective gulped—a grimace of disgust spreading across his chubby features.

"Why? Why the hell would you murder and rape an innocent girl like Eden?"

I shrugged my shoulders. "The girl was irrelevant. She just happened to be a naïve dumbass bitch but," I paused and grinned, "she sure had a tight pussy. James wasn't lying about her virginity. We busted her until our cocks turned bloody."

"You twisted, sadistic piece of shit! I oughta break your fucking jaw!"

I held my hands up in protest. "Whoa! What's with the hostility, detective? I'm only telling you what happened in my own words. Isn't that what you wanted?"

He ground his teeth but allowed me to continue.

"As I was saying, we glorified Satan and believed that by committing the ultimate crime against God— killing a virgin in other words—it'd somehow earn us a one way ticket to Hell. You know, it says in the Bible that in the end Lucifer will bring out his best in everything—music, love, murder . . . "

The man raised his caterpillar eyebrows, still fuming.

"Sounds like bullshit to me, boy. But anyhow, you'll rot in jail till you die."

"I don't think so." I leered at him.

The detective opened his mouth but no words emerged.

"The story isn't quite over yet. Shall I continue?"

He sniffed, then waved his hand.

"You're going away for murder. We have all the evidence we need. But humour me, punk."

I scratched my chin, inviting memories back in.

"Several weeks after Eden's demise, James collected us and we all drove to old eucalyptus grove."

"It's your turn to dig her up this time, bro," James ordered, tossing me the shovel.

She was buried right beneath the surface—just like Randy wanted. We ogled the decomposing corpse. It fucking stank! Still, the boys wanted a bit of fun. Randy unzipped his pants—eager as usual. Then James.

"Your turn, Jason."

Don't ask me why, but out of nowhere—I realized the perversion of the situation. The state of the corpse repulsed me.

"I ain't touching her, James."

He seemed surprised.

"What do you mean you ain't touching her? She's still wet!" he laughed and pointed.

I spat, crossing my arms—defying our leader.

"*If you're not with us, you may no longer exist –* just like the Slayer song says," James threatened.

"Fine. Turn her around for me, I want to do the bitch from behind." I said—giving in.

"Attaboy!"

James grunted, struggling with the dead weight.

"Hey Randy! Gimme a hand, will ya? She gained a few pounds or something."

Randy obeyed without hesitation.

The truth is, after killing Eden—I itched to repeat the experience. Slaying her awoke a dark addiction. I *needed* to kill again. Someone, anyone.

My grip tightened on the shovel and I whacked James over the head before he could react. Randy twitched, but I swung at him too. He dropped like a leaf, cradling his broken face.

Both lay unconscious beneath my feet, at my mercy. I had none.

I chopped at their necks with the shovel like a savage—severing flesh from bone. Then, I pissed all over their corpses, tossing them into the rotting hole. I dug up a fresh grave for Eden—far away from the two little cunts.

I paused my tale.

"You see, detective, they killed her for the music but I killed them for *me*. Because I felt *alive*. Forget ganja, forget meth—killing is the ultimate drug. I suggest you remove your gun and shoot me now . . . or there will be others. I can't stop. Hell, humans are the bane of this planet. The death of three more won't make much difference."

His odious eyes flicked to mine.

"You'd like that, right? An easy way out? Think again. You'll suffer—that's a fucking promise! You're looking at a life sentence, kid. Did that sink in yet?" His mouth formed a gloating smile.

"I don't give a shit. I'm dangerous to other humans. Death follows in my footsteps and people will *die*—so kill me now if you want to save lives," I said.

"No. I want you to stand trial and face your crimes like a man. Look all those people in the eye—the sons you killed, the girl you slaughtered like a lamb— you'll face them all and experience their hate. After that, you'll rot in a tiny cell—getting bum-raped, you sick fuck."

I fell silent for a second, contemplating his empty threats. He gloated, as if his words had some profound effect on me. When I failed to respond to his provocations, he leaned over to me—sliding a bunch of documents under my nose.

"Date and sign here," the detective prompted, offering me his ballpoint.

I admired the pen for a moment—its metallic edge. Sharp. Lethal in the right hands.

"Just sign the papers, will ya?"

When his eyes wandered, the killing urge invaded my limbs and I exploded like an alligator—jabbing the pen into his thick neck. I hit the jackpot and blood sprayed on my face, table and walls. Bathed in blood like *Carrie* in that legendary scene, where the bucket of pig's blood pours over her head—I watched the fat piece of shit die.

Ecstasy rushed through me as he choked on his own vomit, very much like Eden. Our eyes met. "I warned you there'd be others! You should've listened, pig!" I screamed. Slipping the gun out of his holster, I circled him like a starving coyote.

"Since you lacked courage to shoot me yourself when I asked you to, I guess I will have to do it myself! We must cleanse the Earth . . . " I proclaimed, pulling the trigger.

Akona

"HAT HAVE you done with my baby?" she yelled. Her spittle flew and crash-landed on my cheek. Reflex made me blink while little balls of tears formed in Amber's eyes.

"I don't know. She was there one minute and gone the next," I replied with my palms raised as if she held me at gunpoint. My neck burned from the intense Peruvian sun as Amber continued to verbally assault me.

"How could you leave her? She's just a toddler!"

"I was right there behind that tree," I pointed at one of many Palmettos in the area. "And I needed a wee so badly!" A pathetic attempt at defending myself, I know.

We had met at Greenwich University and dated for three months. Amber had a baby daughter, Akona, from a previous relationship. I hated kids and knew nothing about them. I didn't want to learn either.

She invited me to Peru as a part of her Conservation & Biodiversity study. We decided to turn it into a mini holiday, taking Akona with us. It was Amber's idea, by the way, not mine.

"You irresponsible bastard, I should've never trusted you with her!"

Amber had been out on a lecture that morning so we scheduled a picnic for that same afternoon. I got the basket ready and she agreed to meet us by the Ucayali River. I had unrolled a little blanket on a small patch of clean grass and left Akona to play on it – only for a few minutes - as I relieved myself nearby. It never occurred to me that something dangerous might happen to her.

Was she snatched by someone?

We were surrounded by a tribe of simple-tons. . . why would they take her? Shit, maybe they were a cannibalistic tribe.

"She probably just crawled off," I weakly offered. Amber stared at me with her mouth hanging open.

"Don't worry. I'll find her. I'm sure she's around here somewhere," I said.

"Akona! Akona!" I called out, half-expecting her to emerge from the bushes wagging her butt with a stick in her mouth.

I dived into the nearest bush, frantically searching for the baby girl. Nothing. I plunged into the next one but again, found nothing.

I heard soft rustling behind me.

"Amber! She's here behind these plants," I cele-brated prematurely.

I spread the leaves apart and tripped over some-thing, landing face first into the bush. Then I gasped. The head of an enormous *Eunectes Murinus* or the green Anaconda as it's more commonly known, was staring right at me. I must've tripped over its body.

It was huge! But that's not what shocked me. The reptile was in the middle of devouring Akona; only her tiny feet could be seen dangling from its unhinged jaw. We both screamed.

The Green Tide

HE TIDE was low when we arrived at the beach. A stretch of sand like no other we'd visited before—this one was special. The things that lived here were special. That's why I brought her here, my French girlfriend, Cerise. For years, she pestered me about visiting France and meeting her parents. We dated for seven years and I never met her parents. I suppose I felt intimidated by her privileged background and the constant fear of not being good enough.

Her folks were into private schooling, career building, and all that jazz. I assumed them to be the kind of pretentious people that judged a person by their education rather than natural intelligence or strength of character. Still, despite our differences in upbringing, I loved her. Our sense of humour was identical and she made me laugh like no one else could. Also, she was loyal to me—or so I thought.

One summer, I decided to make more of an effort by arranging a weekend getaway to Brittany. Her folks lived somewhere in that region and I promised her we would finally pay them a visit. But first, we would stop at the beach. . . where the green things lived.

We chose a secluded spot for our sunbathing, far away from the plebs and their screaming offspring. I spread the towels on the sand and watched her strip down to her bikini. She had an amazing body. Cerise lay on her belly while I sensuously rubbed lotion into her creamy skin. She moaned softly, "Dat feelrz so nice," her French accent still strong. I kept my eyes on her back but my attention soon shifted towards the sea. The killers were here.

"Fancy a dip?" I asked innocently after several minutes.

Cerise whipped around, smiling playfully.

"Sure! Let'z go," she replied, and reached for my hand.

"You go in first," I offered. "I'll join you in a minute. I want to soak up some more rays."

She smiled once more and I anxiously watched her feet sink into the mud.

"Eww! The sea smellz of rotten eggz!" Cerise complained.

Chuckling, I closed my eyes, reminisced back to the day when I first learned she was sleeping with her boss. I ignored it for years, trying to reason with myself it might not be true, but I was unable to keep my demons at bay. One evening, I gave in and checked her cell phone. I found dirty messages and plenty of them. It must've gone on for months. She hadn't even made the effort of deleting them.

Anyway, the time of reckoning had come. I only had one hobby since childhood. Botany. The only thing

I ever excelled at. I was an expert when it came to plants and weeds.

In my early years at the university, I was intrigued to discover that seaweed could generate toxic fumes of hydrogen sulphide when it rots, a colourless and highly poisonous gas—which incidentally smelled of *rotten eggs*.

Armed with this knowledge, I carefully plotted Cerise's demise. This area of Brittany was renowned for killer seaweed incidents. Several animals had died here a couple of months ago and if my presumptions were correct, small pockets of hydrogen sulphide were still trapped in the beach mud. Hopefully, they'd escape when disturbed.

Cerise called from down below, "Arrre you coming den?"

"In a little while, you keep walking and enjoy the swim!" I replied.

Pins and Needles

HE MOON reposed in the night sky, illuminating the factory's cluttered car park. A polished, liquorice-coloured Mercedes circled it like a serpent. After an interval, the motorist triumphed and wedged between a Mazda and a rusty old Peugeot. Key turned and the ignition died. The shadowy driver bowed his head—sighing. A change of profession blessed him with a fresh start, yet he felt jittery.

Glancing at the object swinging from the rear view mirror, he brushed his rumpled fingers against it, muttering words in a foreign tongue. More cars whisked round the curve, blazing radiant lights and stealing his vision, temporarily. He released the token and gathered his rucksack. The man stepped towards the factory's ominous doors.

"Hey! Send Andy down here, will ya? One of the machines stopped again!" John hollered, his ears ringing from the manic industrial noise. The mushy ear defenders irritated him. The mechanic nodded and John veered around, eagerly heading to the canteen. Glancing at the time, his stomach rumbled and he wondered what Sharon had packed for dinner.

John snatched a bag from his locker and strolled through the canteen door. He spotted Andy, a colleague and a dear friend relaxing in the corner—munching on fries and reading a naval book.

"What you doing here? You had your break, didn't you?" John said, collapsing into a vacant seat. He opened his plastic food container, then stared at Andy's ketchup-drowned fries.

Andy groaned and slammed the novel down. Interrupted reading bugged him. Mike barged in, holding a pot of hot tomato soup in his remarkably hairy hands. He grinned and headed over to the table. Andy shifted over to the other chair.

"Hey Mike, how's it going?" Andy asked, gesturing towards the empty seat.

Mike put down the sizzling pot and leaned closer. A sly smirk spread across his chubby cheeks. "Got news for you, gentlemen. Have you been introduced to our new supervisor yet?"

Both men exchanged surprised grimaces. Andy spoke first. "We have a new supervisor? Since when?"

Mike sipped his soup, blowing at the steam. "Since today. Oh, and John? You definitely won't approve of him."

John swallowed a mouthful of peanut butter sandwich, sneaky crumbs still hiding in his beard.

"Why not?"

The door slammed open and a robust figure appeared. The man's oval face seemed even darker under the canteen's bright lights. He sported a mocha raincoat and clutched a tattered rucksack, decorated with outlandish symbols. Swollen blood vessels altered the natural colour of his eyes.

The black man strolled towards the trio, his stride slow and lazy.

"You must be da mechanics; I are now in charge of you. Ma name is Imamu," he said in a Haitian accent.

Andy sliced the awkward silence in half with his extended hand.

"Hello! I'm Andy and this is Mike and John."

"Evenin'," said Mike, also shaking hands with the new authority.

John's hostile expression communicated without words. Imamu sensed the bearded man's animosity and jabbed him with a red glare. John refused to break eye contact at first, but shifted his gaze eventually. He failed to endure Imamu's trance-like stare. He grabbed his empty container and brushed past the intimidating stranger, cursing.

The changing room stank of oil and sweat. They found John in a furious state of mind.

"I'm not going to bow down to THAT!" he raged, slamming the rusty door of his locker. "I refuse to take orders from his kind. I'd rather quit. Did you hear him talking like he owned us? Who the hell does he think he is? He's just a stupid jigaboo!"

Andy and Mike swapped disapproving glances. John was a racist with a short temper—common knowledge in the factory. Due to his many years of service, the management turned a blind eye. John often rambled but his senile mind wasn't capable of inflicting harm. Or so they thought.

Andy observed the buzzing mechanism. He reached down to his cluttered toolbox—then twitched. A pink palm handed him a wrench. Andy took it, startled by the frowning face.

"Ya friend does not like me," Imamu said.

Andy wiped oil off his hands with a stained cloth.

"I do apologize for my friend, he means no harm. It just takes him a while to get to know people, that's all."

The supervisor remained frigid. "Lies! This note was taped to ma locker," he said, dangling a piece of paper in front of Andy, "and let me tell ya now, boy, I do not take lightly to threats—especially from a racist bigot!"

Imamu's red pupils flashed with menace and Andy swallowed, not doubting the conviction behind the man's threat.

The apparatus roared to life and Andy yelled, victorious. It had taken him over an hour to diagnose and fix the problem.

He chucked the wrench in the box and removed his safety goggles. Mike zigzagged between the machines, arms waving and rushing towards him. His pale face betrayed him.

"What is it?"

"It's John. . . he had an accident," Mike panted.

"What accident? What are you talking about?"

Andy killed the machine, allowing Mike to regain his breath.

"John was operating the cutting mill," Mike said, choking back vomit. "It caught his sleeve and dragged him in. The blade sliced his left arm off like a chunk of ham! Blood sprayed my face! There was blood everywhere—it was horrible! I heard his screams over the noise and killed the power! A second later and he would be dead!"

"Where is he? Which hospital? I gotta see him!" Andy said. Mike grabbed him by the collar, his hands trembling with adrenaline.

"Wait! You know who's to blame, don't you? That damn spear-chucker! I've seen him creeping behind us, watching everything we do! He's plotting against us! I'm telling you, we're next!"

Andy stared, wild eyed. Mike's accusation seemed farfetched. Yes, the supervisor disliked the trio due to John's hostile letter, but to suggest he was responsible for the accident was absurd.

"Don't be ridiculous!" he said, shoving Mike's hands aside. "Did you witness Imamu forcing John under the machine? We can't just go around and throw accusations at innocent people! This whole accident thing will be investigated by the company, you know? Do you really want to be the one pointing fingers and spreading silly theories?" Andy asked.

Mike blinked and lowered his voice. "There's something I haven't told you. When I arrived this evening, I was parking my Nissan and saw him leaving his Merc, heading towards the factory. I went over to check out his ride. A couple of weird and random objects lay inside. The one that disturbed me the most, though, was a voodoo doll—suspended from the rear view mirror. I'm telling you, this guy is some sort of a witchdoctor and I know he caused the accident. . . somehow."

The incoming week, the company scheduled a meeting and launched an investigation into John's mysterious accident. As the only witness, Mike carefully stated his version of events. He detailed rushing over when he heard John's screams—seeing his severed arm jammed in the contraption and then running for help. He considered reporting his suspicions about Imamu, but Andy persuaded him not to—still championing the man's innocence.

Andy and Mike slipped into their boiler suits, depressed. The aftermath of the accident still weighed heavily on both men. It clouded the factory's melancholy atmosphere even further. The doors swung open and the colossal frame of Imamu strode in. He paused, observing his employees with burning hate. Mike and Andy exchanged worried glances. The coloured man resumed his stride.

"You think we should apologize to him? Clear the air a bit?" Mike said.

"Damn right we should! I'm glad you finally accepted the truth. Look, we work a graveyard shift.

We're all naturally tired and John was simply a victim of his own clumsiness. Imamu is innocent. By the way, did you know that John taped a racist letter to his locker?"

Mike's jaw dropped.

"Exactly. We should be *grateful* to him. He could've taken the letter directly to human resources and they would sack him. He done John a favour, you know?"

They entered the factory floor, searching for Imamu. The machinery was on standby and a mild humming ruled over the premises. The men found their quarry sitting on a steel bench, filling out documents. He lifted his crimson eyes but did not offer a smile.

"Sir?" Andy began.

Mike risked a brief visual inspection of the man while Andy spoke, noticing the peculiar amulet hanging around Imamu's gargantuan neck. The amulet had a wooden mask in the centre, its edges decorated with what appeared to be human teeth. Mike averted his eyes, shuddering.

". . . we just wanted to apologize for John's hostile behaviour and we ourselves haven't exactly been very welcoming, so if we could perhaps start over?" Andy said, offering his hand again and grinning sincerely. The supervisor's hesitation filled the air with boorishness. He shook Andy's hand after an awkward pause.

"No problem, ya guys! Give ma best to ya friend, eh?" he replied, clicking his pen.

The shift ended and Mike yawned, feeling extremely tired. It seemed the factory's recent tragic event had stripped him of vitality. He bumped into Andy outside, smoking and leaning against a wall.

"Can I bum one?"

Andy removed a pack of smokes from his pocket and passed it to Mike.

"That was one shitty shift," Andy said, the fumes exploding from his nostrils.

A spotless black Mercedes rolled out of the car park, stopping beside the two men. The electric window slid down.

"Ya got a second, friend?" Imamu said, but his features remained hidden in shadow.

Mike glanced at Andy and approached the car, reluctant. He levelled with the window and found Imamu's murky eyes.

"Just to make ya guys aware, da overtime will be available from tomorrow night. Ya know, if ya or Andy are interested?"

Mike listened, his eyes touring the interior and resting on the swinging doll. His pupils dilated and the black man chuckled.

"Give John ma best wishes, eh? Hope to see him real soon!" With that, he stepped on the accelerator and shot off—knocking Mike off balance.

Transfixed, Mike gazed at the fast disappearing automobile. Andy stubbed out the fag, burning his fingers on the falling ash. He joined Mike and slapped his shoulder.

"Oh! I almost forgot to tell you! I visited John in the hospital this morning, questioning the letter. Well, he claimed he never wrote one. Typical John, huh?"

Still puzzled, Mike blinked—his mind vacant.

"What did Imamu want?"

"The doll had a pin in its left arm. . . " Mike whispered to himself.

Andy bit into his knuckle, a vain attempt to calm the fury that raged within. "That son of a bitch."

"You know what this means, don't you?"

"Yeah, you were right—that coon was behind it all along. Poor John! We gotta avenge him! Hey, fancy a game of cricket tonight?" Andy said.

"You bet."

The cherry red bonnet of Mike's Nissan reflected the luminous satellite. In the reflection, it almost looked stained, as if fused with blood. They arrived early, hoping to ambush Imamu in the car park like silent assassins, lurking in the shadows. Speed was essential. A swarm of ample blows, that's all. In and out.

Andy leaned against the door, lighting a cigarette. Mike tapped his fingers on the steering wheel, eying up the cricket bat on the seat next to him. Perspiration trickled down his armpits.

"Hey! Turn off the fucking lights! I think that's him!" Andy hissed, crouching and exhaling smoke.

The shiny Mercedes pulled into a bay, two rows in front. They waited, hearts pumping with adrenaline.

The door swung open and Imamu stepped out, stashing something into the pockets of his raincoat.

"Ready?" Mike whispered.

Andy nodded, retrieving his bat from the Nissan. Mike glanced around the car park one last time. No one in sight. They creeped towards the dark figure.

"Is this ya plan then? A few blows widda wooden stick? Iz that all ya friend is worth to ya?" Imamu chuckled, his back not yet turned.

They froze. How did he see them? How did he *know*?

Andy gathered his wits. "That's right, coon. You gonna pay for what you did to John with your mumbo-jumbo."

"Careful, boy! What I did to ya friend waz just a beginning!" Imamu said, pulling out another doll from his pocket.

Mike whimpered at the sight of it. It resembled Andy.

"Ya think ya little stick can harm me?" Imamu continued.

Andy clenched his jaw. "We'll find out, won't we?"

He swiped at Imamu, but the bat never reached its target. Andy yelled in pain and crumbled to the ground, cradling his broken leg.

The weapon slipped from Mike's clammy grasp. His eyes rested on the doll and its twisted leg. How it connected to Andy's body he did not know.

"You goddamn ape! You'll pay for this!" Andy cried.

Imamu stared in silence. Then he snapped the doll's neck and Andy spoke no more.

A warm sensation alerted Mike. He glanced down at his urine stained trousers.

"Please, don't hurt me!" he begged.

Imamu reached into his other pocket, pulling out another humanoid figurine.

Mike trembled, retreating. Imamu snapped an arm and Mike dropped to his knees—screaming.

"Why? Why did you do this to us?"

Imamu levelled with Mike, gazing into his soul—wallowing in his pain.

He shrugged his shoulders. "Ya kind has oppressed ma people for centuries. So why not?" he said, tearing the doll's head off.

Dear reader,

We hope you enjoyed reading *Amaranthine and Other Stories*. Please take a moment to leave a review in Amazon, even if it's a short one. Your opinion is important to us.

Discover more books by Erik Hofstatter at https://www.nextchapter.pub/authors/erik-hofstatter

Want to know when one of our books is free or discounted for Kindle? Join the newsletter at http://eepurl.com/bqqB3H

Best regards,
Erik Hofstatter and the Next Chapter Team

You might also like:

Christmas Evil by Mark L'estrange

To read first chapter for free, head to:
https://www.nextchapter.pub/books/christmas-
evil

Story Notes

The Birthing Tub

This is the most recent (and fun!) story in the collection. We all have parasites living, feeding and multiplying inside of our bodies. I don't know about you, but just imagining that appetizing scenario scares the shit out of me (pardon the pun, I assume you read the story so you'll know what I'm talking about). It frightens me far more than your ghosts, vampires, werewolves etc. Why, you ask? I'll tell you why. Because it's *real*. It can actually happen. To any one of us, including you or me. These tapeworms can grow to monstrous lengths, we're talking 20, 30 metres. I wouldn't want that coming out of my asshole, would you? No. It's disgusting but more importantly—it's *scary*. Perhaps not in a traditional sense of the word, but scary nonetheless. If you're familiar with my previous work, you'll know that I favour realistic horror. Human suffering. The torment of everyday life. And writing a story about an intestinal parasite just seemed like a logical step in the right direction (well, I was drunk and it seemed like a good idea at the time!). So there you have it. A story about a tapeworm. But that wasn't enough. Even I knew that a tapeworm wouldn't make much of a relatable protagonist. So I outlined a concept of a heartbroken man, attempting to adjust to his newfound loneliness by creating a special. . . friend. We all reach a point in our lives when we feel alone in the world and we all react differently. But we all want to be loved. You might reach out to your parents, siblings, sons or daughters, cats or dogs, but what if you had absolutely no one to reach out to? What then? Perhaps Eli would become your only friend, too.

Tristan's Equation

When I was a kid, I sucked at maths. And I still suck at it to this day. I guess the cool thing about being a writer is that you can create characters who will overcome any obstacles you throw at them, whilst you observe from the comforts of your sofa or a chair. So I decided to create the opposite of my childhood self. A kid who's not only good at maths, but is a fucking mathematical genius! Ah, the joys of writing! Conjuring characters that excel at everything you never did. Loser. And that's how Tristan was born. But again, to inject that little bit of human trauma into it—he doesn't remember any of it! Due to an accident, he lost the ability to create new memories so he's stuck in this limbo, not knowing why or where he is. Again, I personally find that kind of realistic horror very frightening! The Millennium Prize Problems is a real thing, by the way. The Clay Mathematics Institute is truly offering a $1 million prize to whoever provides the correct solution. Fancy having a go?

Amaranthine

A few years back, I read an article (and you might remember this because it's not that long ago) where books bound in human skin were discovered at Harvard University. For some odd reason, my mind immediately sprang to *Necronomicon Ex-Mortis* (Book of the Dead from the *Evil Dead* franchise, but originally a story by Lovecraft). As a huge fan of the original trilogy, I decided to pay homage with my own little tale! My story wouldn't invoke any demons, roaming around the woods. Instead it would focus on the disturbing factor of binding books in human skin—pure and simple. So I started researching anthropodermic bibliopegy. I was shocked to learn that this thing was actually pretty popular back in the day (waaaaay back in the day!). I created another loner, who inherits an antique bookshop from his father. Struggling to keep the business alive (and also yearning for an everlasting token that he could touch and *feel*) he decides to revive the ancient trend. It follows a similar theme as the other stories in this collection. This "art" existed. Perhaps it still does. Realistic horror, remember? As morbid as it sounds, I thought the idea was worth exploring. I'm telling you, there are plenty of weirdoes out there (why you looking at me?) who would jump at the opportunity! Forget cremation. Forget ashes. Forget urns. When the time comes, I'm planning on using my dad's skin to bind my own books. He just doesn't know it yet.

The Wandering Pilgrim

Rasputin. I've been fascinated by this mystical figure for many years, especially his renown influence over Alexandra Feodorovna (wife of Nicholas II, the last Tsar of Russia). I originally wrote this piece for *Flash Masters 2*—a flash fiction contest organised by *Grey Matter Press*. The rules dictated a length of 250 words. I gave it a shot and the story won a Reader's Choice category. Not bad, eh? Still, I thought it would benefit from a little expansion. Obviously, this isn't quite horror. Rasputin's reputation included an insatiable lust for power and debauchery. So I rolled with that. Again (and you'll be sick of hearing this by now) I attempted to keep the "realistic" horror element present by having a character, who sexually exploits a woman under hypnosis. Losing control of our own mind and body is a frightening prospect. As with the other stories, hypnosis is *real*. Now look into my eyes. . .

The Deep End

I have very little recollection of this tale and the inspiration behind it. It's my least favourite story in the collection. *Manor House Show* bought it and recorded an audio version that did surprisingly well. I suppose if I plunge into the deepest depths of my memory (see what I did there?) it was inspired by a Slovakian au pair my friend once dated. Apparently, she was full of entertaining stories that included washing her employer's shit-stained boxers. How we laughed. So I created an au pair named Eva, who moans about the British culture and the family she works for. Then I threw a spoiled, jealous child into the mix. I sidestepped the realistic horror approach on this one (boo!) and included a mythological creature called *Morgen*. It was loosely based on the Welsh/Arthurian legends. The *Morgens* (similar to *Sirens* from the Greek mythos) lure men to their deaths with their beauty and visions of underwater gardens, built from gold and silver. Granted, you probably won't find one of them in a pool in your local leisure centre—but I thought it would be fun to try anyway! My intention was not to give too much away, therefore the appearance of *Morgen* remains obscure (all the reader "sees" are strands of hair, floating in the drain at the bottom of the pool). The story has a speculative ending. Make of that what you will.

Eucalyptus Grove

This is an odd one. It's loosely based on the Elyse Pahler murder. Three teenage boys lured their friend to eucalyptus grove, to hang out and smoke weed. Then they wrapped a belt around the 15-year-old girl's neck and stabbed her to death. Why did they commit such an atrocity? Because they were devotees of the heavy metal band *Slayer* and believed that they needed to offer a "sacrifice" to the Devil—to give their own garage band the craziness to go professional. With this particular story, I had to tread very carefully for many reasons. After weeks of writing and re-writing, I decided to scrap it. I just couldn't find the right angle. Months later, I had a conversation with Lisa Knight (editor of my first collection, *Moribund Tales*). She asked to read the story and encouraged me to revive it. I wanted to make it clear that the two boys killed her for the music, but this third guy developed a thirst for blood (no, not like a vampire—you douche) and couldn't stop thinking about killing again. In the end, he overpowers the detective and mutters: "We must cleanse the earth." Then a gunshot. Did he shoot the detective or himself? Ah, that would be telling! As a fan of *Slayer*, I found this story incredibly tragic and gruesome. It got me speculating about how influential music can be. Scary, when you think about it.

Akona

Akona is the middle name of my partner. I know what you're thinking, what kind of a twisted idiot names a baby after his girlfriend and then lets a giant anaconda eat it? Yeah, that's me. I sold this one to *The Literary Hatchet* for a very reasonable fee (considering the puny length). Here comes the realistic horror speech again. Anacondas. Fascinating and monstrous creatures, right? Very real. An average sized anaconda could easily kill an adult person (so tiny infants are like popcorn to them). My girl visited Costa Rica and explained all about the fabulous creatures she encountered on her trip. I listened with enthusiasm but personally, I wouldn't fly anywhere near South America (my mindset is similar to Karl Pilkington). I changed the setting of the story from Costa Rica to Peru, but it's all the same climate really. When people ask me whether I like children (not in that way) I always point them to this story. These snakes simply scare the living crap out of me (maybe because I was far too young when I watched *Anaconda* with J.Lo). So yeah, there you have it. I dedicate this story to all the anacondas out there (and no, I'm not talking about giant dicks—sorry, ladies).

The Green Tide

Another one of those stories half inspired by an article. Several years ago, there was a supposed incident on the beaches of Brittany, where holidaymakers were warned against a "killer seaweed". Apparently, it was as poisonous as cyanide and reported that 28 wild boars died when they breathed in a toxic gas, released by the foul-smelling algae as it decomposed. It's normally found on most northern French beaches, but it releases hydrogen sulphide when it comes into contact with nitrogen waste, flowing to the sea from the pig and poultry farms. They claimed that a council worker on a seaweed clearing team was poisoned by gas and taken to hospital in a coma. A local marine biologist warned that this gas was very toxic and smelled like rotten eggs. He said that it attacks the respiratory system and can kill a man or an animal in minutes. Mind you, I think I've read the column in Mail Online so it was probably a load of shite. Still, it immediately captured my attention and I thought it would make a cool story. Did I mention realistic horror? Yeah, something like that. So the guy, a botanist—brings his cheating girlfriend to this beach, secretly plotting her demise by using the poisonous seaweed. Again, the ending is speculative. Will she survive? Will she die? You decide. I managed to sell it to *Theme of Absence* for a token payment and the story received positive feedback. Not from my girlfriend, though. For some reason, she wasn't keen on this one.

Pins and Needles

Years ago, when I was still studying creative writing, I wrote a short story entitled *The Needle Factory* for one of my assignments. To be honest with you, I never liked it. The dynamics were all wrong— so I scrapped it. I had no intention of publishing this story. . . ever. But when I decided to put the collection together, I went through all of those hidden and forgotten piles of paper buried at the bottom of the drawer. And there it was—staring back, mocking me. I read it again. . . and loathed it even more. There was a spark in there somewhere, but whipping it into shape would be extremely difficult. I groaned, unsure what to do with it. Luckily, my friend Karen Runge (a fellow horror author) came to the rescue. She read it and gave me some feedback. I ripped the story apart and did a complete rewrite. As suspected, it was bloody hard work! The plot is quite controversial, obviously racism being the main ingredient. But still, it's also a good old-fashioned voodoo story and I hope people will enjoy it for what it is. Again, I drifted from the realistic horror theme with this one. Voodoo dolls (and the entire philosophy behind them) intrigued me for years, though, so it had to be done.

About the Author

Erik Hofstatter is a schlock horror writer and a member of the Horror Writers Association. He dwells in a beauteous and serenading Garden of England, where he can be encountered consuming copious amounts of mead and tyrannizing local peasantry. His work appeared in various magazines and podcasts around the world such as Morpheus Tales, The Literary Hatchet, Sanitarium Magazine, Wicked Library, Tales to Terrify and Manor House Show. 'Rare Breeds' is due to be published in March 2016 by KnightWatch Press.

You can find out more about Erik and his writing at http://www.erikhofstatter.net/

Or follow him on Twitter @ErikHofstatter and Facebook at

http://www.facebook.com/erikhofstatter

Lightning Source UK Ltd.
Milton Keynes UK
UKHW021101021120
372650UK00004B/599